Wherever you roam there's no place like home. Wherever you roam like home. Wherever you roam there's no place like home. Wherever there's no place like home. Wherever you roam there's no place like home.

A Special thanks to
my publicist Dorothy Finn
for her dedication towards
the success of this book,
to Marie Puerini
for additional editing,
thanks to Lakuna
for designing all my books,
and many thanks to
Peter Martin
for my website,
I can never thank you enough.

PUMA....PUMA...HERE KITTY, KITTY........PUMA....... PUMA... WHERE ARE YOU?

Library of Congress
Copyright office
101 Independence Ave., S.E.
Washington, DC 21559-6000

Published and Illustrated by Muriel Barclay de Tolly

Book Design, Editing and Additional Illustration - Lakuna Inc. / Newport, RI

PUMA, LOST IN NEWPORT

by
Muriel Barclay de Tolly

This is a story about
a little girl, named Brigitt;
her wandering cat, Puma;
and Mima -The grandmother
that loved them both.

The continuation of

Where's Puma?

Puma was a cat with a sense of adventure,
and today she would set out
on her biggest journey.
She slipped out the door and was on her way
to see the sites of Newport.
The history, the people, the harbor,
and the Mansions.
Little did she know she was about to become
the talk of the town.

Mima- it's Brigitt,
Puma is nowhere in sight.
I'm so worried, what should I do?

Brigitt don't worry. I'll have Art
down at the radio station make
an announcement and Captain Joe
send out some police cars.

Mima,
I just got a call!
someone just saw a
black and white cat in
Touro Park, I sure hope it's her.

.....this is Art Bellutti... on WADK.....look out for a black and white cat!
........her name is PUMA and she belongs to a little girl named Brigitt

Puma loved Touro Park.
There were lots of people to watch,
trees to climb, and a mysterious stone tower.
Puma wondered what the tower was for, and
how it was built.

She was so relaxed and happy in the park,
that she forgot about one thing..
...dogs...no cat likes dogs....so off she
sped, to find safer ground..

Woof.....Woof.....woof

Woof.....Woof.....woof

Brigitt, this is the Preservation Society, we think we've spotted Puma in one of the mansions. She looks as if she's hiding from something.

Puma knew that a mansion was a giant house
but The Elms mansion was even
bigger than she had thought.
It was like a castle, and had a beautiful
sunken garden, perfect for a
game of hide and seek.
She felt like a queen strolling around
the yard, and thought about how great
it would be to live there.
She would throw big parties, and
stay in a different room each night.
No noise...no dogs....
oh no.... no Brigitt!
it could never feel like home
without Brigitt.

Brigitt, It's Aunt Katie. I was jogging by the Newport Bridge, and I thought I saw Puma in Battery Park. Could it be her?

The Newport Bridge was the biggest
bridge Puma had ever seen, and way on
the other side was Jamestown.
Jamestown sounded like a
nice spot to visit,
but today it was a little out of her reach!
Instead she watched the boats go by.
Then she was off to
see some old familiar spots.

Mima... the Rabbi just called.
He was sure he saw
Puma on the lawn of the Synagogue.

Touro Synagogue was right around the
corner from Mima's restaurant, Muriel's.
Puma had been there many times before.
She loved to watch the
people visit the Synagogue,
and today she learned that Touro was the
first Jewish Synagogue
in the United States.

Puma's tummy started to grumble,
so she ran back to Muriel's for a snack,
but there was nobody there.

Well then, where to next? she thought.

Brigitt... this is Mr.Coffee
from the gas station
I can see Puma, she's in front of Muriel's.
Oh wait...Oh no.. there she goes!

Thank you so much for
helping out.
I've gotten so many calls about Puma.
She's become the most
talked about cat in town.
Wait. Can you hold?
Someone's on the other line....

Brigitt... this is Julia the Hairdresser.
Puma just ran by my store
and across the street to city hall.

Puma ran to the steps of City Hall where
she thought she saw Brigitt,
but it wasn't her.
She started to think about home, and how
she couldn't wait to share her day.
But she wasn't ready for home yet!

Mima,
the Ida Lewis Yacht Club just
called. They think they saw Puma
walking up the dock.
When will she come home?

Puma had heard so much about the
yacht club and Ida Lewis, the heroic
women it was named after.
Many years ago Ida Lewis had saved
so many people out of rough seas,
she became a legend.

It was getting late and Puma was
beginning to feel that she had
been gone for too long.
She thought about the places
she still wanted to go to,
but she only had time for one more stop.

Where would it be...

... fire station # 5 to visit the firemen who got her out of a tree the day she decided to get a better view.....

....or the Tennis Hall of Fame to chase some balls.....

...how about a little skate down at the rink..

...or some good treats like Mima gets from the Market....

...or maybe she could get Brigitt a new dress....

Puma started to feel a little overwhelmed and perhaps a little lost. Then she spotted the coffee shop that Mima always goes to, and that made her think of Brigitt, then she knew exactly where she wanted to go....

...but then.....

Mima,
the Police Station called.
They have Puma, in a police car
on her way home.
I'll be so happy to have her back.
What a day it has been!

When Puma got home she thought back
about the places she had been and
the sites she had seen,
and she smiled because she knew she
was in the greatest place in town......
home.

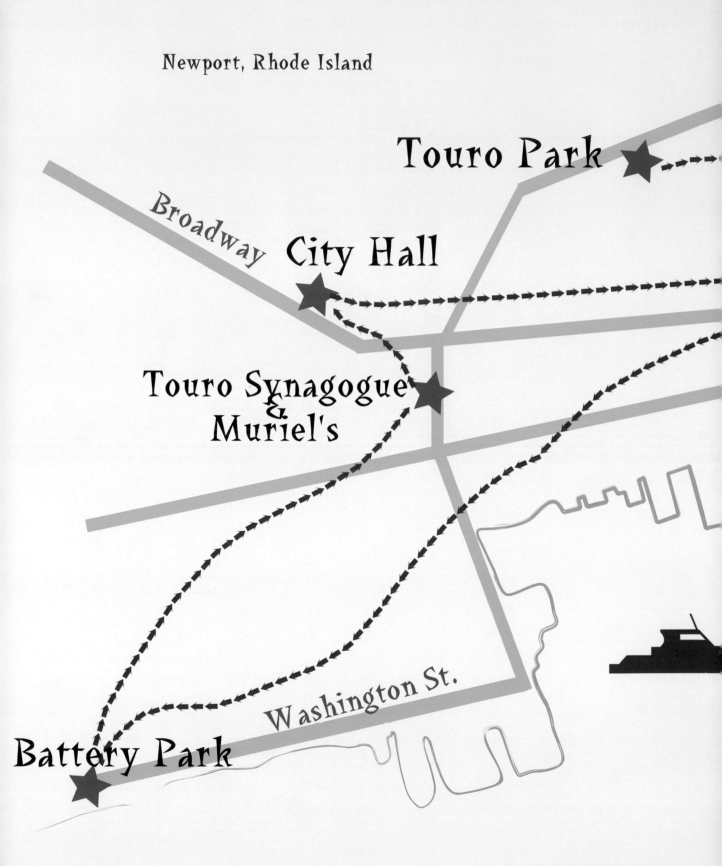

Newport, Rhode Island

Touro Park

Broadway

City Hall

Touro Synagogue
&
Muriel's

Washington St.

Battery Park

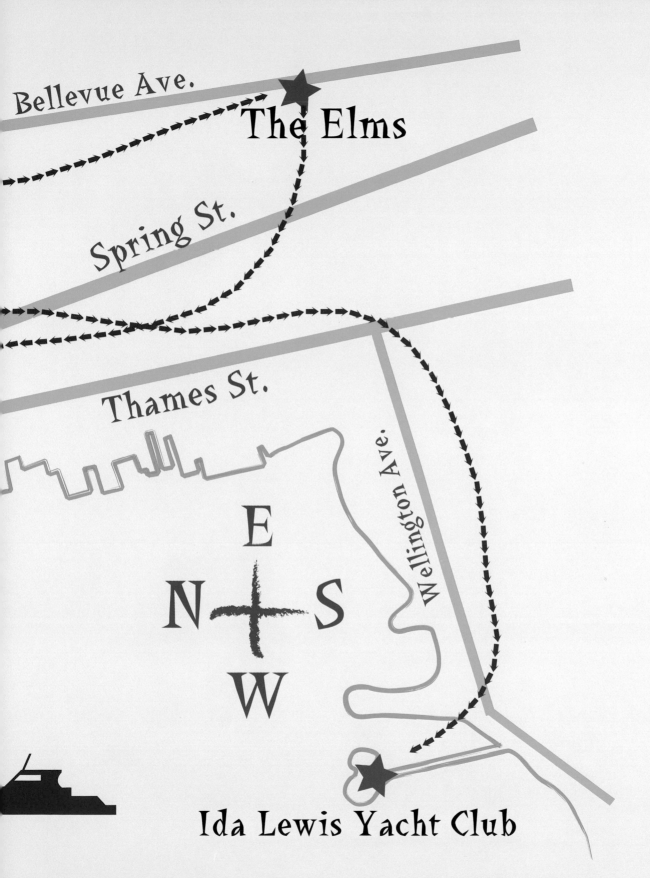

Bellevue Ave.

The Elms

Spring St.

Thames St.

Wellington Ave.

E

N + S

W

Ida Lewis Yacht Club

A million thanks to my whole family for their support!

Muriel Barclay de Tolly (Mima)

Mima's Family

Also by Muriel Barclay de Tolly:

Behind Newport Doors Cookbook,

Behind Newport Doors Cookbook Too,

and Where's Puma?

For information

www.murielofnewport.com

Puma still resides in
Newport, Rhode Island
"the city by the sea."